All Change

by

Rosie Rushton

Illustrated by Ros Asquith

YA FF

1250353

First published 2001 in Great Britain by
Barrington Stoke Ltd
10 Belford Terrace, Edinburgh EH4 3DQ
Copyright © 2001 Rosie Rushton
Illustrations © Ros Asquith

Reprinted 2001, 2003

ISBN 1-902260-75-9
Printed by Polestar AUP Aberdeen Ltd

A Note from the Author

This is not a true story. But then, it's not a made up story either. It's about a girl who thinks she has to pretend to be something she isn't just to get the guy she wants.

That girl was me. I was once so busy trying to be someone else that I almost forgot who I really was.

But like Jemma, I got my happy ending.

This story is for everyone who is still trying to be the best thing they can be - THEMSELVES.

For Lorraine and Deborah with thanks
and admiration

Contents

Chapter 1
I'm Out of Here!

Have you ever had one of those days when your whole life changes because of one tiny, little thing? If I hadn't had a blazing row with my Mum that Thursday, I might still be the same old boring Jemma Jarvis. I might never have got a life.

But that was the afternoon that Mum told me the news. She and Colin, that dweeb she lives with, were actually going ahead with their crazy idea of selling up and moving to the other end of the country. And what happened after that turned my whole life upside down. Forever.

It had been a day from hell at school. When I got home my Mum had this big grin on her face like she had just won the Lottery. She grabbed hold of me and twirled me round the kitchen like some mad woman.

"We've bought the cottage in Norfolk! They've accepted our offer! Isn't it exciting?" she cried.

"You've done WHAT?" I gasped in disbelief. Mum and Colin had been talking about moving for months, but I never thought they would be daft enough to do it.

"I knew you would be thrilled!" laughed Mum.

Thrilled? I was horrified. And she didn't even notice.

"No more traffic jams, no more noise!" she went on. "Just fresh air and wide open spaces!"

Well, I ask you. Who in their right mind wants to swap two big shopping malls, a multi-screen cinema and a cool nightclub for a lot of muddy fields and a village with only one shop? "You're mad!" I shouted. "I won't go. You can't make me!" I pushed her away and stormed towards the door.

Biting gnat

Land (flat)

sheep (fat)

cow   pat

Yokel's hat

Mud splat

To THIS?!

"Oh, Jemma, do be a bit more reasonable!" she replied. "Anyone would think that I was about to whisk you off to some desert island!"

"It might as well be a desert island," I shouted. "I mean – Norfolk! Just miles of sand dunes and that crummy, old cottage!"

They had dragged me there a couple of weeks before and believe me, it was grotty. The floorboards creaked, the doors didn't shut properly and the garden was full of stinging nettles.

Mum sighed. "But darling, the cottage will be lovely once Colin has done it up," she said. "And besides, the boys will have a fantastic time there!"

Well, that did it. "Oh, well, that's all right then, isn't it?" I yelled, yanking open the kitchen door. "As long as your darling, little boys are happy, I can go to hell! Well, stuff that!"

I slammed the door behind me. My eyes had filled with tears and I almost fell over a toy dump truck as I ran down the hall.

I know it sounds a bit over the top, but I really felt as if I couldn't take any more. It had been the same ever since my twin brothers were born. It was as if I didn't exist – everything in Mum's life centred around Sam and Ben. Who had to move bedrooms so that they could have a bigger one? Me. Who couldn't play music in the evenings in case the twins woke up? Me.

And now, worst of all, my entire life was about to be turned upside down so that the boys could live by the sea and eat stupid organic vegetables.

"Hateful kids!" I screamed, kicking a couple of toy cars out of the way.

Mum stormed into the hall after me. "Jemma, come back at once!" she shouted after me. "You're being childish and stupid!"

"Oh, really?" I spun round to face her. "My mother leaves my Dad, takes up with a guy young enough to be her son, has twins and then decides to move to some dump in the middle of nowhere and it's ME who is supposed to be the stupid one?"

"That's enough!" she cried.

For a second, I thought she was going to burst into tears, but she just clenched her fists tightly, took a deep breath and sat down on the bottom stair. She gazed up at me with a pleading expression on her face. "Look," she said, "once you get to Norfolk and settle into the sixth form college there, you'll enjoy it. It will be a whole new life for all of us."

"I don't want a new life!" I replied. "I want the old one back! The one we had before you messed it all up."

Maybe I shouldn't have said that. I mean, Dad wasn't exactly a saint and Mum did try to keep things together for years before they split. But I wasn't feeling tactful. In fact I felt rotten. My period was due and my stomach felt like a cannonball about to explode. "You just don't care, do you?" I went on. "You're so selfish! First you leave Dad and now you expect me to go off to Norfolk and leave all my mates behind! You even expect me to be pleased about it."

Mum closed her eyes and ran her fingers through her hair. "Your friends can come and visit," she said. "And anyway, you're not leaving anyone special like a boyfriend behind, are you?"

That did it. She didn't have to rub it in. I've only ever had one boyfriend and that was when I was twelve. It's not that I'm ugly or anything – I'm just not the sort of girl that boys go for in a big way. Or any way at all, come to think of it. I've learned to live with it.

But I didn't need Mum to remind me. "Oh, really?" I yelled, turning away and pulling open the front door. "No boyfriend? Well, that just goes to show how little you know."

Why I said that I will never know. It just came out. Mum's face was a mixture of shock and disbelief but I didn't stop to look for long. I just ran down the path and out onto the street.

"And just where do you think you are going, young lady?" Mum called after me.

"I'm off out!" I yelled but by then I was trying so hard not to cry, that my words just came out as a high-pitched squeak. I did not know where I was going and I wouldn't have told her anyway. Let her worry, I thought, as I ran across the road. Let her imagine me sobbing for hours in a bus shelter. Let her feel guilty. She deserves it.

"But it's raining!" she called. "You haven't got a coat!"

"So what?" I snapped.

To be honest, I hadn't noticed the rain but there was no way I was going back now. No way at all.

At that moment I decided to go to Lisa's house. She's my best mate and I knew she would be furious when she heard how Mum and Colin were planning to ruin my life.

Once I had made up my mind, I couldn't wait to get there. I could have gone all the way round the streets to get to her house, but I decided to take the short cut straight across the park.

And that's where it all began.

Chapter 2
Oh Wow!

By the time I was halfway across the park, it was pouring with rain, but I didn't care. I just kept running. I was so angry that I felt I might explode. "I hate them, hate them, hate them!" I muttered over and over. My feet pounded along the path to the beat of the words.

That was when the amazing thought struck me. I didn't have to go to Norfolk at all. I knew my rights. I was sixteen years old. You are allowed to leave home at sixteen and do your own thing. I could go and live with Lisa! Her Mum had a spare room now that Lisa's brother was married. And she was always saying she didn't see enough of me.

I could be free! Free of screaming toddlers, manic mothers, best of all, free of Colin! The whole idea blew my mind so much that I stopped dead in my tracks and gasped for breath.

And at that very moment, something crashed into my back and knocked me sprawling, face down, onto the muddy path.

I screamed and got a mouthful of wet leaves.

"Hey, are you OK?" said a deep voice behind me.

I rubbed a lump of mud from my left eye, spat out the leaves and looked up.

And that's when it happened.

I fell in love.

Just like that.

I know what you are thinking. You are thinking that love at first sight is something that only happens in films. Well, it's not.

You are thinking that when you fall in love the world doesn't really stand still, everything doesn't really go all golden and sunny and you don't really see little, pink hearts everywhere.

Well, you do.

OK, not the pink hearts bit.

But when I looked up and saw these two huge, brown eyes gazing down at me, I knew that this was *it*.

He was to die for. He was tall and suntanned. He had dark hair that stuck to his forehead in little damp curls and a little drop of rain hung from the end of his nose. He was clinging onto the trunk of a small tree as if his life depended on it. "I'm really sorry," he said, in a husky voice that sent shivers of ecstasy down my spine. "I haven't quite got the hang of stopping yet." He pointed to his feet and I realised that he was wearing rollerblades. "Are you hurt?" he asked.

I opened my mouth but nothing came out. It was as if my whole body was frozen. My heart was thumping and my legs felt like jelly.

"Can you get up?" he went on. He sounded worried. He bent down, grabbed my hand and pulled me to my feet.

"Thanks," I whispered. His hand was warm and smooth and I rather hoped he would never let go.

But as soon as I was standing up, he dropped my hand and staggered back onto the path. He turned and looked at me. I pushed my wet hair out of my eyes and tried to look laid back. That's not an easy thing to do when you're wearing school uniform and no make-up and when you're covered in mud from top to toe.

ARE YOU OK?

"You're soaked!" he said. "Don't you have a coat?"

I shrugged my shoulders. I hoped I was looking cool.

"I like to feel the rain on my skin," I said and wanted to kick myself for sounding so dumb.

He nodded. "I know what you mean," he said. Which was amazing, because I hadn't a clue what I was talking about.

He bent down to tighten the lace on one of his boots. I knew he was about to go.

"Is that hard?" I asked quickly. "Rollerblading, I mean."

He grinned. "The blading bit is easy," he laughed. "It's just the stopping that's difficult!"

"Can I have a go?"

I didn't want to have a go. In fact, the thought of having a go terrified me, but I would have stood on my head if it had meant I could keep him near me for a bit longer.

He laughed and shook his head. "The boots are far too big for a titch like you," he said. "And besides, I'm in a hurry."

"Right," I said. "Titch indeed. I'm five foot three and a quarter."

He stood up and looked me over rather more carefully. "Well," he said, "I guess that apart from looking like a drowned rat, you're all in one piece."

I should have said something witty. Or sarcastic. Or just plain sexy.

But I didn't. "Don't worry," I said. What a stupid thing to say.

"Right," he replied, spinning round on one rollerblade. "Well, I must go – I'm late for work already." And with that he skated off without a backward glance.

I stood there in the rain and watched him speed off down the slope towards the boating lake. His gorgeous little bum wiggled as he bladed from side to side. I gazed as he stumbled and stretched out his arms to regain his balance.

I imagined what it would be like to have those arms wrapped around me. Just thinking about it made me feel quite faint.

That was when I knew I had to see him again. There was only one problem – I didn't have a clue how I was going to make it happen.

Chapter 3
And This Is What We Do ... !

Luckily, Lisa was alone in the house when I got there. Her Mum's great but I was in no mood for polite chat and a chocolate biscuit.

"What on earth have you been doing?" Lisa demanded to know, pushing me upstairs to her bedroom. "You're filthy!"

"I've fallen in love!" I said with a sigh.

"Fallen in the mud? I can see that," frowned Lisa, raising her voice above the music pounding from her room.

"No, I've fallen in LOVE!" I shouted. "Well, in the mud as well, as it happens."

Lisa pushed open her bedroom door and shoved me down onto her beanbag. Then she turned down the stereo and stood over me, hands on hips.

"Jemma, what are you on about?" she demanded.

I sighed. "I've met this amazing guy," I began. Lisa opened her eyes wide.

"OK, you don't have to sound so surprised!" I snapped. "Just because I don't get through six boys a term like some people I could mention!"

Lisa grinned and sank down on the floor beside me. "So – go on!" she urged. "Tell me about it!"

So I told her the whole story – how I was in the park and how he crashed into me and took my hand. And how his eyes crinkled when he smiled and how I just had to see him again.

"Wow!" breathed Lisa. "That is SO romantic! So what's his name?"

I swallowed. "I don't know," I admitted.

"You don't know?" Lisa yelled. "You mean, you didn't ask him?"

I shook my head.

"Well, where does he live? What school is he at?"

I shrugged my shoulders. "Don't know,"

I said again.

Lisa scrambled to her feet and glared at me. "Jemma, you're mad! You meet a gorgeous guy and then you let him get away! You don't have a clue about pulling a boyfriend, do you?"

"It all happened so fast," I said sadly. "I guess I've blown it. I'll never see him again."

Lisa sounded annoyed. "You can't just give up!" she said. "Go on, tell me again what he said."

"He knocked me over, asked if I was OK and told me I looked like a drowned rat," I began.

Lisa giggled and nodded. "Well, you do."

I ignored her. "And then he said he had to go because he was late for work," I finished.

Lisa's mouth dropped open. "Work?" she asked.

I nodded.

"Well, that's it, then!" Lisa cried. She clapped her hands and seemed very excited. "Don't you see? That is *it*."

"What is what?" I asked.

"We find out where he works and then we go and check him out." She looked really pleased with herself.

"Oh, sure!" I replied in a sarcastic tone. "Dead simple. There must be loads of places in town where he could work. Get real!"

Lisa glared at me. "Look," she said. "Do you fancy this guy or don't you?"

"Yes," I said sulkily.

"Do you want to see him again?"

"Of course I do."

"Then go for it!" she shouted.

I nibbled on my thumbnail. "But where do we start?" I asked her. "The town is full of offices and shops."

Lisa grinned one of her smug, I-know-better-than-you sort of smiles. "But he doesn't work in town," she declared.

I stared at her. "And how do you know that?" I asked.

"Because you told me you watched him rollerblade past the boating lake," she said proudly, "which means he was going in the wrong direction for the town centre."

I was impressed. "You're right!" I nodded.

"I usually am," she grinned. "So this is what we're going to do."

She perched on the edge of her dressing table. "Tomorrow after school, we go to the boating lake and we wait. With any luck, he goes to work by the same route every day. So we get to see him!"

I frowned. "But what if he doesn't come?"

"Oh, for crying out loud, Jemma!" Lisa snorted. "What's the matter with you? Why do you always look on the black side of everything?"

I bit my lip and my stomach turned over. For just a few moments, I had forgotten that my whole life was in ruins. "Even if he did turn up," I muttered, "there would be no point getting to know him. We're moving."

Lisa's mouth dropped open. "You're what?"

"Moving," I said glumly. "To Norfolk. Mum and Colin have bought that cottage I told you about."

"But that's awful!" she said and flung her arms around my neck. "You're my best mate. You can't go. I'd miss you so much!" She was really upset.

"Well," I said nervously, because that is not how I'd planned to tell her this. "There is one idea I have had. Something that might mean I could stay."

"Of course!" Lisa exclaimed. "This guy! If you can get it together with him, anything could happen!"

That wasn't what I had meant, of course. I had been about to ask about moving into

Lisa's spare bedroom. But when she put it like that, with her eyes shining, I almost believed that anything was possible.

"That settles it!" declared Lisa, before I could protest. "You and I are going to make sure that this guy falls for you in a big way. OK?"

I was about to remind her that guys and me don't go together, but she looked so excited that I didn't have the heart. "OK," I grinned. "Let's go for it."

"Great," she grinned back. "And by the way, Jemma?"

"Yes?"

"Wear something sexy, OK?"

I didn't think I had anything remotely sexy in my wardrobe, but I knew better than to argue with her. "Yes, Lisa," I said. "Of course, Lisa. Whatever you say."

Chapter 4
Disaster!

When I got home, Mum was all smiles again. She didn't yell at me for running off and she didn't ask where I had been. She didn't even grumble about the mud on my skirt. I knew why. She wanted to find out whether I really did have a boyfriend.

Of course, she didn't ask me straight away.

First of all, she told me she had made fried chicken for supper, which she knew was my most favourite food in the whole world. Then she said she was going to give me an extra £1 a week on my allowance. And then, of course, she said what she always says when she is itching to know my secrets.

"You do know, darling," she said sweetly, "that you can talk to me about anything. Anything at all. You do know that, don't you?"

I gave her my most angelic smile. "Yes, Mum," I said. "I do."

She waited. But all I said was, "Shall I lay the table, Mum?"

She gave a deep sigh. "I've already done it," she said rather sharply. "Go and wash your face. You look a right mess."

****

"I still look a mess, don't I?" I asked Lisa when we met up outside the park the following afternoon.

"No," said Lisa, but she didn't sound very sure.

"Do you think my bum looks too big?" I pleaded. I ran my hand over my capri pants and peered in Lisa's mirror.

Lisa took a closer look. "Well ..." she said and then grinned. "Only teasing! Come on — let's go for it!"

We got to the boating lake at exactly five o'clock and sat on one of the benches near The Parking Place café.

We were still sitting there at a quarter past five. We were still waiting at half past. By a quarter to six, I'd had enough.

"He's not coming," I said miserably. "It was a dumb idea anyway."

Lisa sighed. "Perhaps he's got a day off," she said. "Perhaps someone gave him a lift. We'll try tomorrow. Come on, I'll buy you a milk shake in the café to cheer you up."

I didn't want a milk shake. I was too miserable to breathe, never mind drink anything. But Lisa ignored my protests and dragged me through the door.

"There's a table," she said. "Over there by the window."

I looked across the room. And gasped out loud. My knees went all weak. My mouth went dry and I could feel my cheeks burning. "Oh, my God," I whispered.

"Now what?" grumbled Lisa.

"That's him," I gasped, "he's serving that old couple in the corner."

Lisa turned round.

"Don't look!" I hissed out of the corner of my mouth. "Isn't he divine?"

"How can I tell whether he's divine or not, if you won't let me look at him?" she replied.

"But he might see us," I said in a panic.

"I thought that was the idea," she replied. "Come on!" She grabbed my hand and pulled me to the vacant table. "Excuse me!" she called out brightly as the guy walked past. "Can we order?"

The guy turned round.

"Sure," he said. "What will you have?" He pulled out his notepad and looked straight into my eyes. "Hey!" he said. "Aren't you the girl I ran into yesterday?"

I nodded. I was so happy to see him again that I couldn't find a word to say.

Lisa kicked me under the table and pulled a face at me. "Say something," she mouthed silently across the table.

"Are you any better at stopping yet?" I said in a high voice.

He laughed. "Sadly, no," he grinned. "I almost fell over a small poodle today! Now, what will you have?"

You, I wanted to say. All I want is you. "A raspberry milk shake, please," I murmured.

"And a chocolate one for me," added Lisa.

"Coming right up," he said and disappeared into the kitchen.

"Isn't he divine?" I breathed. "Don't you think he is the most gorgeous guy you have ever seen?"

Lisa shrugged. "Not my type," she said. "But he's OK. And at least you know his name now."

"No, I don't," I said.

"Oh, Jemma, don't you ever notice anything? His name was written on his badge. *Tim Fraser – Here To Help You.*" She giggled and gave me a nudge. "And we all know what sort of help you would like from him," she grinned. "Now all you have to do is find out when he finishes work – and be here!"

She made it all sound so simple. At that moment, he came back carrying our milk shakes.

"Well," he said, looking directly at me, "that's me finished for the day. What a way to earn a living!" He pulled off his apron. "Are you sure that I didn't hurt you yesterday?" he said, touching my shoulder.

I felt as if a thousand volts of electricity had shot through my body. "Sure," I whispered.

"Great!" And with that, he gave a brief wave and headed for the door.

"Drink up!" hissed Lisa. "Fast! We need to follow him!"

I took a huge gulp of ice-cold milk shake and began to splutter and cough. A dribble of pink milk shake trickled down my T-shirt.

"Oh, very sexy!" grumbled Lisa. "Just leave it! Come on!"

As we reached the door, the guy on the till called after us. "You haven't paid!"

Lisa hurled some money at him and stood tapping her foot as the guy searched for the right change.

We ran outside.

"There he is!" Lisa cried, pointing along the path. "Sitting on that bench by the swings! Now think of something dead cool to say to him."

"Like what?" I asked.

"Do I have to do everything for you?" she demanded. "Just something that will make him want to get to know you better. He's interested, you know."

"He is?" I found that hard to believe.

"Sure thing," said Lisa. "He touched you – that's very promising. He's probably sitting there now, hoping that he'll see you again soon." She put her hand in her jacket pocket and pulled out a pound coin. "Now run after him with this and say he dropped it," she said.

"But he didn't," I protested.

Lisa closed her eyes and sighed. "I know that," she said, "but he won't be sure. It gives you something to talk about."

I took the coin. "Aren't you coming with me?" I asked.

"Get real!" she said. "He's not going to ask you out with me standing there, is he?"

I gulped. "Do you think he might? Ask me out, I mean. Do you think there's a chance?"

Lisa raised her eyebrows. "Not if you stand here much longer!" she said. "Now get on with it!"

I took a deep breath, flicked my hair behind my ears and walked towards him. He didn't notice me. He glanced at his watch and stood up.

I walked a bit faster. I couldn't lose him now. Then he sat down again. Go for it, I told myself. "Hi," I said as brightly as I could. "You dropped this." I thrust the coin into his hand.

He frowned. "I don't think it's mine," he said. "You keep it."

"No!" I gasped. "I mean – it's not mine. You take it."

He paused, staring at me for a long time. "OK," he said with a grin. "Thanks." He slipped the money into his pocket. "I'll buy you a drink next time you're at the café," he said.

Next time. He wanted there to be a next time. Lisa was right. He was interested.

I thought my heart would burst with joy. I sank down on the bench beside him. "OK," I said, trying to sound as if I really couldn't care either way. "When?"

He didn't answer. He was staring over my shoulder and his cheeks were turning pink. He stood up, running his fingers through his curly hair.

"Timmy!"

I spun round to see a tall, graceful girl hurrying along the path towards us. She had shoulder-length black hair and a figure to die for. She was wearing a bright pink strappy dress and wacky floral mules and looked as if she had spent all day getting her make-up just right. Even her fingernails were perfect. Each one was painted a different colour.

"Shelley! Hi, gorgeous!" said Tim and his voice sounded quite different. "What kept you?"

The girl tossed her head, pouted her lips and planted a kiss on his cheek. I wanted to kill her. "I chipped my nail polish just as I was coming out," she said. "So I had to start all over again." Shelley slipped her arm through Tim's and glanced at me. "And who is this?"

She made me feel like a small insect that had crawled out from under a log.

"Oh, this is Jenny," Tim said.

"Jemma actually!" I spat out my name.

"I knocked her over when I was rollerblading," he added.

Shelley nodded. "Ah, now I understand," she said scornfully, her eyes fixed on the raspberry coloured stain on my T-shirt. "At first I thought she looked like that on purpose."

Tim frowned and looked at me. "Oh, no," he said, "It happened yesterday."

"Really?" Shelley sneered. "So what's her excuse today then?"

Tim chewed his lip and looked embarrassed. But he didn't say a word. He just peeled the paper off a strip of chewing gum, shoved it in his mouth and slipped his arm round Shelley's shoulder. "Let's go," he said briskly. "Bye, Jemma."

I didn't reply. I was too busy trying not to notice the way Shelley nuzzled his neck and made pathetic kissy-kissy noises. It made me feel sick. It should have been me.

Then suddenly, he turned round and stared at me. He opened his mouth and then closed it again.

"Come on!" ordered Shelley, pulling his hand. "I'm getting cold!"

I rather hoped she would freeze to death on the spot, but since it was July and the sun was shining, I didn't think she would.

Tim looked at me for a moment longer and then turned and walked away. I knew what he was thinking. He was thinking what a total loser I looked beside the oh-so-wonderful Shelley.

I stood there and watched them as they strolled along the path, Shelley's head on Tim's broad shoulder. Then I turned and plodded back to where Lisa was waiting. It wasn't until she thrust a grubby tissue into my hand that I realised I was crying.

Chapter 5
The New Me!

"That does it!" Lisa cried slipping an arm through mine. "You are going to get that guy and what is more, I am going to make sure you manage it!"

I shrugged my shoulders and tried to look as if I didn't care. "No point with Shelley around," I said. "What chance do I have against Little Miss Perfect?"

"Little Miss Perfect," replied Lisa, "is a cow. A two-timing, double-crossing, totally hateful COW!"

I gazed at her. I was amazed. "You mean, you know her?" I cried.

Lisa nodded. "She stole Darren away from me last year," she replied. "Remember?"

I frowned. Lisa had so many boyfriends. But I did remember one last autumn, about three boyfriends ago. He'd suddenly dropped her and she'd been really upset. That could have been Darren.

I nodded, just to be on the safe side.

"Her name is Shelley Hall," spat Lisa. "She lives opposite me and she thinks she's so special!"

"She looked pretty special to me," I muttered crossly. "Once she came along, I was invisible."

"Well, all that is going to change!" announced Lisa. She grabbed my hand and dragged me along the path. She eyed me up and down with a determined look on her face. "You know what's wrong, don't you?" she demanded. "You look too ordinary."

"Oh, thanks!" I snapped.

Lisa sighed. "I'm only trying to help," she said. "I know about these things. You're sixteen, but you still look like a school kid."

"Well, I can't help the way I look, can I?" I shouted.

Lisa grabbed my arm. "That's where you are so wrong!" she announced importantly. "It's Saturday tomorrow, right? By Monday, you will be so stunning that Tim Fraser won't give Shelley a second glance."

I couldn't help thinking she was living in a dream world. "But what are you going to do?" I asked.

Lisa grinned and tossed her head. "Wait and see," she said. "Just meet me at the shopping centre at nine o'clock tomorrow morning and bring some money."

"Nine o'clock?" I almost choked. "On a Saturday? What about my lie-in?"

Lisa glared at me. "Jemma, what is more important? An extra hour in bed or a future filled with love?"

Put like that, even I couldn't help feeling excited. "OK," I said, "I'll be there."

"Great," grinned Lisa. "Don't be late."

****

Mum nearly fainted when I appeared in the kitchen at half past eight, already dressed. "Darling!" she exclaimed. "I thought you were still asleep."

"I'm going out," I said and grabbed a yoghurt from the fridge.

"Out! Out!" shouted Ben banging a spoon on the table. "Me out too!"

"Out too!" yelled Sam, who copies everything his brother says.

"Out?" repeated my mother.

Honestly, there are times when I wonder if I'm the only one with a brain in this house.

"Yes, Mum," I smiled sweetly. "I'm going out."

You could see Mum biting her tongue and trying not to ask questions. And failing. "Who with?" she said, pretending to be absorbed in the slice of toast she was buttering.

"A friend," I replied. "I've got to go!"

"Jemma! You are not going anywhere until ..." She was about to grab my arm when Sam hurled his mug of milk on the floor and Ben spat Oat Krunchies all over the cat. Mum yelled, grabbed a cloth and forgot all about me.

For the first time since their birth, I was actually glad the twins were around.

****

Lisa was waiting for me by the fountain on the ground floor of the shopping mall. "Right," she said in a business-like manner. "First we'll deal with your hair." She grabbed my ponytail in her fingers and gave it a yank.

"Ouch!" I protested. "What are you doing?"

"That's coming off!" she declared. "It's far too childish!" Lisa marched me across the mall to *Snips*. A sign in the window read 'FENBURY'S LEADING HAIR SALON.'

"I can't afford a place like this!" I gasped. "Get real, Lisa."

Lisa grinned. "It won't cost you much," she said. "My cousin is doing her training here – she will do it for five pounds, just to get experience."

I wasn't too sure that I wanted anyone to get their experience cutting my hair. But you don't argue with Lisa when she is in her organising mood. We pushed open the door and went in.

Half an hour later, the floor around my feet was covered with bits of my hair and my neck felt cold and naked.

"Well?" asked Lisa. "What do you think?"

It certainly looked different. The fringe was a bit wonky and the hair round my ears looked a bit longer on one side than the other. But I did look older. Quite a bit older.

"It sticks out a bit at the back," I pointed out.

"Oh, that will be fine once we've done the rest," said Lisa.

"The rest?" I said. I was getting worried.

Lisa pulled me out of the chair. "Pay the bill," she said, "and follow me."

****

Lisa dragged me up the escalator and into Superdrug.

"What now?" I asked.

"Hair colour," Lisa said. "You simply cannot go on being mousey brown. It is *so* yesterday."

She grabbed a box from the shelf. "What about this?" she asked, thrusting it into my hands. "*Funky Red Flame* – that sounds gorgeous!"

64

"It's red!" I protested. "I can't have red hair!"

Lisa threw the box back on the shelf and turned to face me. "That's your trouble, Jemma!" she snapped at me. "You just don't have a sense of adventure. OK, choose some safe, boring colour – but don't expect Tim to notice you!"

I swallowed. "OK," I agreed. "Red it is. Let's give it a go!"

"Great!" Lisa cried, hurling the *Funky Red Flame* into the wire basket. "Now then – clothes!"

Our next stop was the trendiest clothes shop in town.

"I can't wear that!" I cried as Lisa handed me a snakeprint boob tube. "You must be joking!" I protested, when she picked out a bright pink sequinned top. "I'll look ridiculous!" I sighed, after she made me try on a pair of leather hot pants.

By twelve o'clock we were both worn out.

"You are not leaving this shop until you've chosen something!" Lisa grunted shoving me into Gear Up Girl.

"That's nice," I said, pointing to a long blue floaty dress with spaghetti straps. "But it would show up the zits on my shoulders."

"Oh, for crying out loud!" began Lisa.

"OK, OK," I said. 'I'll try it on."

Half an hour later, we left the shop with the dress. And some funky sequinned sandals. And a karma bead bracelet. Not to mention a cute bag, a pair of wicked drop earrings and a cropped cardigan.

"I'm broke!" I sighed as we slumped down at a corner table in McDonalds. "Mum will kill me when she finds out what I've spent. Not to mention the hair." I ran my fingers nervously over my head.

"Jemma, it's *your* hair and it's *your* life. My Mum says that being a teenager is about discovering who you are."

"Your Mum is normal," I replied. "Mine isn't."

"Leave me to sort out your Mum," said Lisa. "I'll be round tomorrow to colour your hair and ..."

"You can't come to my house!" I gasped. "Mum would never let me do it. I'll have to come to your place. That way she won't find out till it's too late."

Lisa shook her head. "You can't come to mine. Shelley might see you," she said and bit into her cheeseburger. "I told you she lives opposite me."

"So?"

"So we don't want her to know that you and I are friends," she said. "Not until I put our Big Plan into action. I'm not going to let you give it all away."

I sighed. I still wasn't sure what the Big Plan was. "What if all this turns out to be just a big waste of money?" I said. "What if Tim doesn't take any notice?"

"He will," Lisa promised. "But you have to keep well away from the café. And don't hang around outside either. Promise me?"

I looked at her in amazement. "Lisa, you're mad," I said. "He works in the café. That's the only place I'm ever likely to find him. Why would I go to all this effort and then keep away?"

"You just do what I say," she replied. "We have to choose just the right moment for Tim to see the new you. What is the point of going to the café when he's busy working? Or waiting outside if he's going to dash off to find Shelley?"

I nodded slowly. "So what do we do?" I asked, sipping my Coke.

"Leave it to me," said Lisa. "I'm going to pay a visit on Miss Shelley Hall."

"You are *what*?"

"I'll tell her that she's just so lucky to be with such a gorgeous guy. I'll really suck up – tell her I wish I was like her and all that rubbish."

"You're mad!" I gasped. "Then what?"

"Then I'll ask her what she and Tim are doing next weekend."

"Oh, right!" I said. "Like she's really going to tell you that!"

"She will," Lisa said confidently. "She can't resist boasting about how she gets around."

I pushed my cheeseburger to one side. Somehow I wasn't very hungry.

"But I still don't get it," I protested. "Even if you do find out all this stuff, what difference will it make? I need to get Tim on his own, without her around!"

"Will you just trust me?" demanded Lisa. "Have I ever let you down?"

Put like that, I had no choice. "OK," I said. "Whatever you say."

Chapter 6
Lisa Cracks It

Lisa came to my house the next day. First of all she told Mum how young she looked. Then she told her that she thought Sam and Ben were the most gorgeous little boys she had ever seen. She even built a Lego fort for them. She asked Colin to explain the rules of American football and watched it on television with him for a bit.

And then she went in for the kill. "Mrs Jarvis," she said sweetly, brushing her hair out of her eyes, "would you mind very much if Jemma and I used your bathroom? I want to try out a new look and I need Jemma's help."

If *I* had mentioned a new look, my mother would have asked a million questions and gone on for hours about children growing up too fast. Not this time.

"Of course, Lisa dear," said Mum sweetly. "Off you both go!"

The minute the bathroom door was shut, I turned to Lisa. "She will go bananas when she finds out what we are doing," I cried. "You don't know what she is like!"

"Oh, be quiet and put your head under the shower!" said Lisa. "Leave your mother to me."

An hour later we stood side by side in front of the mirror.

"It's very red," I said.

"Mmm," said Lisa. "But sexy."

"And it might fade a bit with washing," I added hopefully.

"Mmm," said Lisa. "Sure to."

Just then, my mother called up the stairs. "Want some chocolate cake, you two?"

We looked at one another. "We can't stay up here forever," said Lisa.

"And at least you are here to stand up for me," I added.

Taking a few, very deep breaths, we went downstairs and into the kitchen. Mum's mouth dropped open when she saw me.

"You see!" cried Lisa brightly before Mum could say a word. "I knew your Mum would be cool about it. She's so together. Great, isn't it, Mrs Jarvis?"

Mum appeared to have lost the power of speech. She just stared at me.

"A lot of mothers would get really

uptight about things like this," Lisa went on, "but your Mum is so cool. You really are lucky, Jemma."

Mum swallowed. Twice. "Have a piece of cake," she whispered.

I waited for her to explode but it never happened. In fact, Mum didn't speak again for hours.

****

I don't know how I got through the next few days. I never stopped thinking about Tim. I dreamed about him every night. I got into trouble at school for not paying attention in class and for writing 'Jemma loves Tim' all over my biology coursework.

My mother kept telling me to keep washing my hair. She said that it would make it shine. She must think I'm daft. All she wanted was the colour out.

I couldn't eat. That was the good bit. I wanted to be slimmer to look good in that blue dress. It was a busy week. On Monday, Lisa insisted that I put fake tan all over my body. By Tuesday, I'd turned a sort of orangey yellow. On Wednesday, she spent the whole lunch break plucking my eyebrows into tiny little lines, which made me look permanently surprised.

Then, on Thursday, Lisa had great news.

When I got to the corner of our street, Lisa was waiting for me, hopping from one foot to the other with excitement.

"I've done it!" she cried, as we crossed the road. "I've found out that Tim is taking Shelley to that new club tomorrow night – you know, The Fallen Angel. It's a teen night. *We'll* be there too!"

"He won't be interested in me if Shelley is there," I began, but when I saw the look on Lisa's face I stopped.

"I'll be round at your house at six o'clock tomorrow evening to do your nails and make-up," she said. "It's going to be most amazing night of your life!"

Chapter 7
He's Mine!

At half past seven on Friday evening, Lisa stood me in front of the bedroom mirror. "What do you think?" she asked. She sounded really pleased with herself.

I stared at myself in the mirror. "It doesn't look like me," I said.

"Well, of course it doesn't!" cried Lisa. "That's the whole idea. This is the new you – older, cooler and much more sexy!"

I swallowed. "Right," I said gazing at my new look. I wasn't too sure I liked the pink eyeshadow and I was even less certain about the lavender mascara. The dress looked cool but I was having a problem balancing on the high-heeled sandals. They had been fine in the shop, but every time I walked across the room I felt as if I was about to topple over. And I really didn't think that black and white fingernails were quite me.

But Lisa was over the moon. She was really pleased with my new image. "He won't be able to resist you!" she declared. "Come on, it's time to go!"

My mother was hovering by the door as I tottered downstairs. "You will look after her, won't you, Lisa?" Mum said, as if I was five years old.

"Of course, Mrs Jarvis," smiled Lisa sweetly.

"I'm not too sure about this club," she sighed.

"It's great," said Lisa. "My Mum never worries if I go there."

Thankfully, Mum didn't know anything about these things. She didn't realise the club had only been open for a week.

"I want you home by eleven!" she called after me. "Don't you dare be late!"

I would have answered, but I was too busy trying to keep my balance on those heels.

****

The evening did not start well. For one thing, by the time we got to the end of the road, my eyes were watering like mad and I could hardly see. "It must be the mascara," I told Lisa. "I've never worn it before."

Lisa peered at me. "Oh, stop making such a fuss!" she snapped. "You will get used to it."

I didn't say anything. But as we stepped off the bus, I made up my mind to go to the Ladies when we got to the club and wipe it all off with a tissue. By the time we arrived at The Fallen Angel, I had something else to worry about. I had twisted my ankle getting off the bus in my high heels and had to limp into the club. What an image. To make matters worse, there was no sign of Tim and Shelley.

"They'll be here soon," said Lisa confidently, as she ordered a couple of drinks. "Just chill out!"

I was still trying to chill at nine o'clock. And at half past. "I knew it would be a waste of time," I muttered as Lisa came back with my third lemonade. "We might as well go home."

"You must be joking!" she replied. "I've got my eye on that blond guy over there.

You watch the door, while I go and chat him up."

"But you've got a boyfriend already!" I protested.

"I'm going off him," she announced. "See you in a bit!" And with that, she pushed her way through the crowded dance floor to the bar.

I felt really stupid. There is nothing worse than sitting at a table in a crowded nightclub all on your own watching other people have a good time. My shoes hurt, my eyes itched and my heart was breaking.

All I could think about was Tim and Shelley. They would be somewhere in town, having a wonderful time, gazing into one another's eyes, kissing and cuddling.

I couldn't stand it any longer. I tried to attract Lisa's attention but she was flirting with the blond guy. I started to push my way across the dance floor. I was determined to drag her away. I couldn't go home alone.

At that moment I looked over to the door and saw a tall, dark figure. It was Tim. At first, I thought I was seeing things. People say that if you want to see someone enough, your brain starts imagining they are there. I blinked. Twice. He was still there. He was peering around the dance floor, shielding his eyes from the flashing lights. Then he turned round and vanished.

For a moment I stood, frozen to the spot. I could hardly believe it. Tim was here and Shelley wasn't. I didn't waste any more time. I just grabbed my bag and ran to the door. I didn't care that it was raining. I didn't care that my ankle hurt like mad. I didn't care about leaving Lisa on her own. All I cared about was catching up with Tim.

Frantic, I looked up and down the street. He was crossing the road, heading for the bus station. "Tim! Wait!" I yelled.

He didn't hear me above the noise of the traffic. I started running after him as quickly as my ankle would let me. I didn't get very far. The heel of one of my sandals got stuck in a crack in the pavement and I fell flat on my face for the second time that week. I was covered in mud again. All over my new dress.

I yanked at the sandal and the heel snapped off. "Stupid sandals!" I muttered. I kicked the good sandal off and ran in my bare feet. It hurt like mad but I reckoned Tim would be worth it.

Luckily Tim wasn't walking very fast and I managed to catch up with him before he reached the bus station. I tapped him on the shoulder. "Hi," I said, gasping for breath.

"Er – hello." He sounded puzzled. Clearly, he didn't know who I was with my red hair and new gear.

"It's me, Jemma," I said, wishing that I wasn't so red in the face. "The park, remember? You ran me down."

He stared again and his eyes widened. Then he burst out laughing, which wasn't quite the reaction I had hoped for. "You!" He almost choked as he said it. "Do you always go around covered in mud?"

I rubbed at my dress and tried to look unconcerned. "I fell," I said. "It was these stupid sandals." I showed him the broken heel.

"Your dress is torn," he said.

"I know," I replied. "I can mend it." This conversation was not going exactly my way.

"And your hair!" he exclaimed. "What have you done to your hair?"

I flicked my fringe and tried to look cool. "I thought a change would be a good idea," I said.

"Well, it was a really bad one!" replied Tim with a frown.

"What do you mean?" I snapped.

Tim turned to me with a guilty grin. "Sorry," he said. "I shouldn't have said that. I'm just not in a very good mood, that's all."

I shrugged my shoulders. "It's OK. I don't think it suits me either," I confessed. "I wanted to look older. I wanted to look cool."

Tim frowned. "I liked you better the way you were before," he said.

My heart missed a beat. "You liked me?" I said and immediately regretted it. Lisa says you must never, ever sound at all interested in what a boy thinks.

Tim nodded. "You were so normal," he said. "And funny."

Normal and funny. That was not the image I wanted. But then again, he seemed to like me like that.

"Explain?" I said.

Tim sighed. "You fell in the mud and you didn't moan on and on about ruining your clothes, or getting dirt under your fingernails. You said you liked to feel rain on your skin."

"That's just as well because it looks as if it's going to rain." I laughed and pointed to the black clouds above us. "I seem to make a habit of chatting away in a downpour."

Tim laughed. "See?" he said. "You're funny." The way Tim said it, it sounded like a compliment.

He sighed. "Shelley – that is, some girls won't even go out in a shower. They say it makes their hair go frizzy."

I took a deep breath. Suddenly it was terribly important that I knew the score. "Is Shelley your girlfriend?" I asked, trying to sound casual about it.

"*Was* my girlfriend," he said.

I wanted to shout and sing and hug him. "*Was?*" I asked, my heart thumping.

He took my arm. "Come on, let's go back to the club and get out of the rain." He held my arm all the way back across the road and into The Fallen Angel. There was an empty table just inside the door and he pulled back a chair for me to sit down. "Shelley and I had a row," he said. "It was my fault, I guess. She kept me waiting again, for a whole hour. Said it was because she had to repaint her nails."

"Oh," I said, sitting on my black and white fingernails.

"Anyway, I told her that I'd had enough and I didn't want a girlfriend who thought more about her looks than she did about me. Selfish of me, I suppose."

"NO!" I cried. I didn't want him to feel guilty about dumping Shelley. "You were right. Quite right."

"I came to the club to see if she was here – just to make sure she was OK," he said.

"That's nice," I said, secretly thinking that Shelley Hall was probably already chatting up some other poor guy. She didn't deserve anyone as caring as Tim.

He didn't say anything for a while. Then he turned and looked at me. "Do you still want to learn to rollerblade?" he asked.

Actually, there was nothing on earth I wanted to do less. "I'd love to," I smiled. "It's something I've always wanted to do."

He grinned. "Meet me in the park tomorrow after lunch at two o'clock," he said. "You can borrow my sister's old blades. OK?"

"OK!" I breathed.

"Want a drink?" he asked.

I nodded. "Lemonade, please," I said.

Tim was at the bar ordering the drinks when Lisa suddenly turned up at our table.

"There you are! I told you he would come! And you're together! I knew it!" She sank down beside me. "So what did he say? And where's Shelley? Gone off in a strop, I bet."

I opened my mouth to reply but Lisa was not listening.

"Why is your hair wet? Has he asked you for a date?"

"Yes, he has actually," I said, trying not to sound too pleased. "He's going to teach me to rollerblade. Starting tomorrow."

"Brilliant!" cried Lisa, giving me a hug. "And you've only got me to thank. I knew that if you had a new image, Tim would

take notice of you. And I was right, wasn't
I?"

I smiled to myself. "Yes, Lisa," I said.
"You were quite right."

"I usually am," she said and sailed back
to the dance floor.

Chapter 8

Who Says There's No Such Thing As Happy Endings?

Tim and I have been together now for four weeks and three days. He has taught me to rollerblade. It's not half as frightening as it looks and I'm actually quite good at it.

I've taught him how to swim underwater, which is cool because no-one can see when you kiss six foot down at the deep end. We go for long cycle rides in the country and he says it's great to have a girlfriend who doesn't mind getting dirty.

I even took him home to meet Mum and Colin. Mum asked him all sorts of stupid questions and Colin talked on and on about football and stock car racing but Tim didn't seem to mind. Mum said he was rather sweet, which is her way of saying she approves of someone. Colin didn't say anything but then Colin doesn't have a brain.

I asked Lisa about moving into her spare bedroom when Mum and Colin went to

Norfolk and she just shook her head. "Why not?" I asked. "Your Mum likes me."

"She likes making money even more," she giggled. "You're too late. She's taken a lodger. She's called Mrs Farmer and she smells of stale cheese."

So that was that. I haven't told Tim I'm moving. I can't bear to think about it. I mean, the people who live in the cottage might change their minds about selling it. Or it might burn down. That part of Norfolk might slide into the sea. Colin might drop dead.

I don't want anything to change. It's all been going so well. Too well, perhaps, which is why I am so scared about tonight.

Tim phoned this morning and said he had something very important to tell me. Something he couldn't put off.

I have a horrible feeling that he is going to dump me. Perhaps he has gone off me now that my hair has gone back to its normal colour and I don't wear masses of make-up or floaty see-through dresses any more.

Lisa was right. Guys want you to have a bit of style. And I haven't got it.

I can't bear to think about losing him. I love him so much. I even thought that maybe he loved me, just a little.

I'm meeting him in an hour. I thought I might dress up in my new gear, but there's no point. I have to be me and I'm just not a high-heeled, floaty dress sort of person.

So I'm wearing my jeans and a cropped top and if he doesn't like it, that's tough.

OK, so I sound brave. I don't feel it. I feel terrible. Maybe I should tell him I'm moving. Get in first. That way, it will look as if I am dumping him. That way it'll be easier to take.

That's what I'll do. It might make me feel better.

He's sitting on the same park bench that he was sitting on that first evening when I gave him the one pound coin. "Hi, Mudlark!" he calls as I rollerblade up to him. That's his nickname for me. Lisa says it is an insult, but I think it's cute.

"Hi," I say and my stomach turns over. "I've got something to tell you."

"Me too," he says. "You go first."

This is harder than I thought. "We're moving," I tell him.

He frowns. "Moving? What do you mean, moving?"

Maybe it's because I feel so uptight, or maybe it's because I don't want to cry in front of him, but I find myself shouting.

"What do you think I mean? Moving house. Moving away from Fenbury. Going away."

His face falls and he looks upset. "Oh," he says and sighs. "Well, maybe that's a good thing."

A good thing? How can moving to a grotty cottage in Norfolk be a good thing? I get it. It's good for him because it lets him off the hook. He doesn't have to feel bad about dumping me. No way, mate.

"So what did you want to tell me?" I ask, feeling more sick by the minute.

He takes my hand and strokes it. "I'm off too," he says. "I heard today."

My stomach flips. "Heard what?"

"I got a place at university," he says.

I don't get it. "But you told me you were fed up with studying," I say. "That's why you didn't go to university last year."

He looks down at his feet. "I lied," he admits. "I did badly at A levels and didn't get a place. But I've always regretted it, so I retook them. And this time I got in!" He looks so pleased I can't help smiling.

"Great!" I say. "Where?"

He sighs. "That's the bad bit," he says. "It's miles away. And I'm going to miss you so, so much."

My heart lifts. "You mean – you're not dumping me?"

"*Dumping* you?" he cries. "I love you, silly. You don't dump people you love."

I throw my arms round his neck. "Then that's OK," I cry. "Wherever you're going, it'll be OK. There are trains and coaches and I can come and visit you."

He squeezes me tight and kisses me for a long time. "You're amazing," he says, releasing me. "Shelley would have cried and screamed at me and said I was a selfish brute."

I shake my head. "I'm not Shelley," I say. "I'm just pleased you still want me. So where are you going?"

"Norwich," he says.

I can't believe it. Did he really say Norwich?

"Say that again," I whisper.

"Norwich," he repeats.

"That's in Norfolk," I cry.

"I know," he mutters. "About as far away from you as I could be."

And now I am laughing. Laughing and crying and hugging him and planting kisses all over his face.

He looks at me as if I have gone mad.

So I tell him. "I'm moving to Norfolk," I cry. "Some place near the sea. Mum and

Colin have bought a cottage."

Now he is laughing and lifting me up off my feet and spinning me round and round. "That's terrific!" he cries. "I hated the thought of leaving you. We can still see each other often," he whispers, nuzzling my cheek. "I'm so glad your Mum and Colin chose to move house just now, aren't you?"

I gaze up into his eyes. "Oh, yes," I whisper. "I've never been so glad about anything in my life."

And it's true.

I think I might even buy my Mum a box of chocolates.

Just to say thank you.

Barrington Stoke would like to thank all its readers for commenting on the manuscript before publication and in particular:

Carolyn Adams
Amanda Armstrong
Kimberley Calder
Hollie Chisnall
Amanda Christie
Rachel Clifford
Gavin Duncan
Lucy Fulford-Smith
Stacy Garson
Alan Gilchrist
Hayley Graham
Lisa Hilson
Margaret Hubbard
Sandra Hughes
Steven Hutton

Gary Jeanne
Sarah Kinnaid
Kirsty McKerchar
Martin Mannara
Kirstin Menelaws
Alice Morey
Kerri Munro
Bob Parker
Tracy Pryce
Steven Raeburn
Stacy Scott
Gemma Smibert
Jonathan Strudwick
Kaya Wills
John Wilson
Alan Young

Become a Consultant!

Would you like to give us feedback on our titles before they are published? Contact us at the address or website below – we'd love to hear from you!

Barrington Stoke, 10 Belford Terrace, Edinburgh EH4 3DQ
Tel: 0131 315 4933 Fax: 0131 315 4934
E-mail: info@barringtonstoke.demon.co.uk
Website: www.barringtonstoke.co.uk

More Teen Titles!

Joe's Story by Rachel Anderson 1-902260-70-8
Playing Against the Odds by Bernard Ashley 1-902260-69-4
To Be A Millionaire by Yvonne Coppard 1-902260-58-9
Falling Awake by Viv French 1-902260-54-6
The Wedding Present by Adèle Geras 1-902260-77-5
Shadow on the Stairs by Ann Halam 1-902260-57-0
Alien Deeps by Douglas Hill 1-902260-55-4
Runaway Teacher by Pete Johnson 1-902260-59-7
The Dogs by Mark Morris 1-902260-76-7